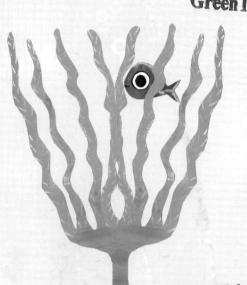

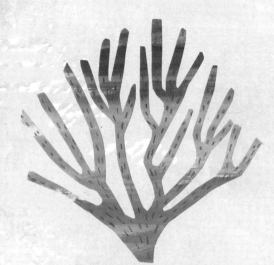

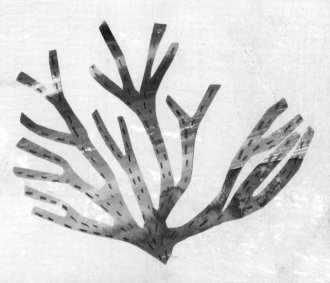

W9-CRQ-314

Received on

NOV 0 9 2021

Green Lake Library

NO LONGER PROPERTY
SEATTLE PUBLIC LIBRARY

To Mum and Dad
—K.R.

Published by
PEACHTREE PUBLISHING COMPANY INC.
1700 Chattahoochee Avenue
Atlanta, Georgia 30318-2112
www.peachtree-online.com

Text and illustrations © 2021 by Kate Read

First published in the United Kingdom in 2021 by Two Hoots, an imprint of Pan Macmillan, a division of Macmillan Publishers International Limited.

First United States version published in 2021 by Peachtree Publishing Company Inc.

All rights reserved. No part of this publication may be reproduced, stored in a retrieval system, or transmitted in any form or by any means—electronic, mechanical, photocopy, recording, or any other—except for brief quotations in printed reviews, without the prior permission of the publisher.

The illustrations were created digitally using a mixture of collage and monoprint.

Printed in May 2021 in China
10 9 8 7 6 5 4 3 2 1
First Edition

ISBN 978-1-68263-327-4

Cataloging-in-Publication Data is available from the Library of Congress.

Kate Read

HEY!
A Colorful Mystery

Ω

PEACHTREE

ATLANTA

All was quiet in the deep, **blue** sea.

Does anyone want to play? said the tiny **pink** fish.

But no one answered.

So...

The rumor grew
bigger **and bigger.**

There are
hundreds
of them!

With mean
thoughts and
big ideas!

To gobble
up all
the fish!

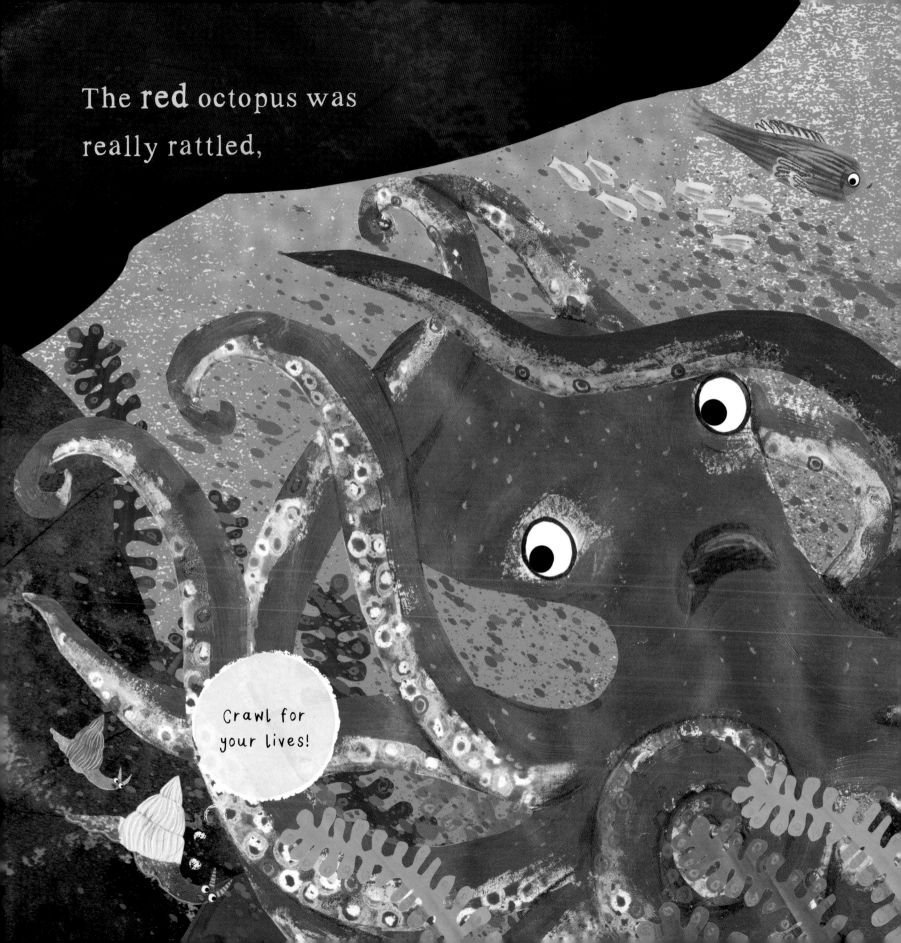

The **red** octopus was
really rattled,

Crawl for
your lives!

which petrified the
purple puffer fish

and startled
the **blue** shoal,

terrifying the
green turtle,

which shocked the **yellow** eel...

and confused the **orange** crabs.

Its claws
are
THIS BIG!

Even the silver-gray sharks were scared.

It has rows of razor-sharp teeth!

The whole ocean
floor shook into
a fizzing, frothing
frenzy, fleeing to...

...the safety
of a deep,
dark cave.

All was quiet in the
deep, dark sea.

said the tiny **pink** fish. And she joined the marvelous, multicolored mayhem.

How to Create Marvelous, Multicolored Mixtures!

Red

Blue

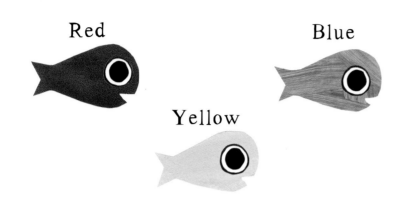

Yellow

Red, Yellow, and Blue are
PRIMARY COLORS.

They cannot be made by mixing other
colors together. All other colors can
be made from just these three.

Orange, Green, and Purple are SECONDARY COLORS.
They can be made by mixing two primary colors together.

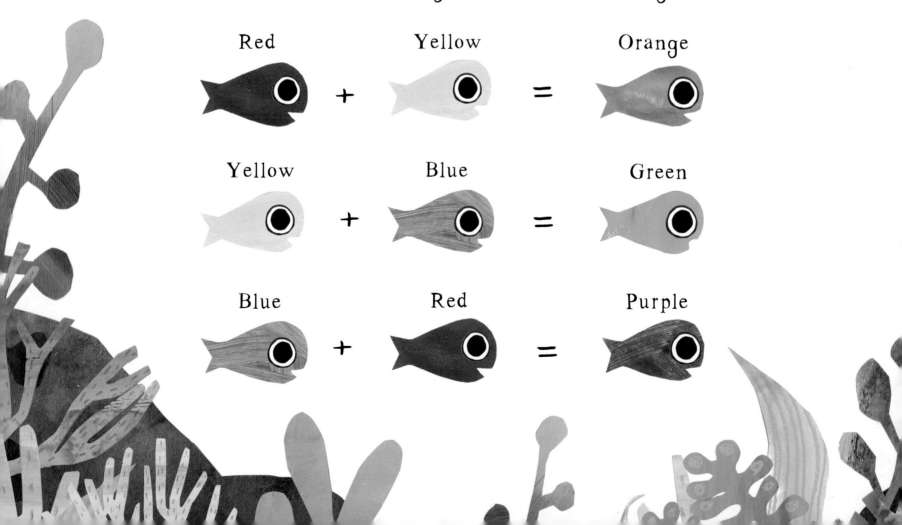

Red		Yellow		Orange
	+		=	
Yellow		Blue		Green
	+		=	
Blue		Red		Purple
	+		=	

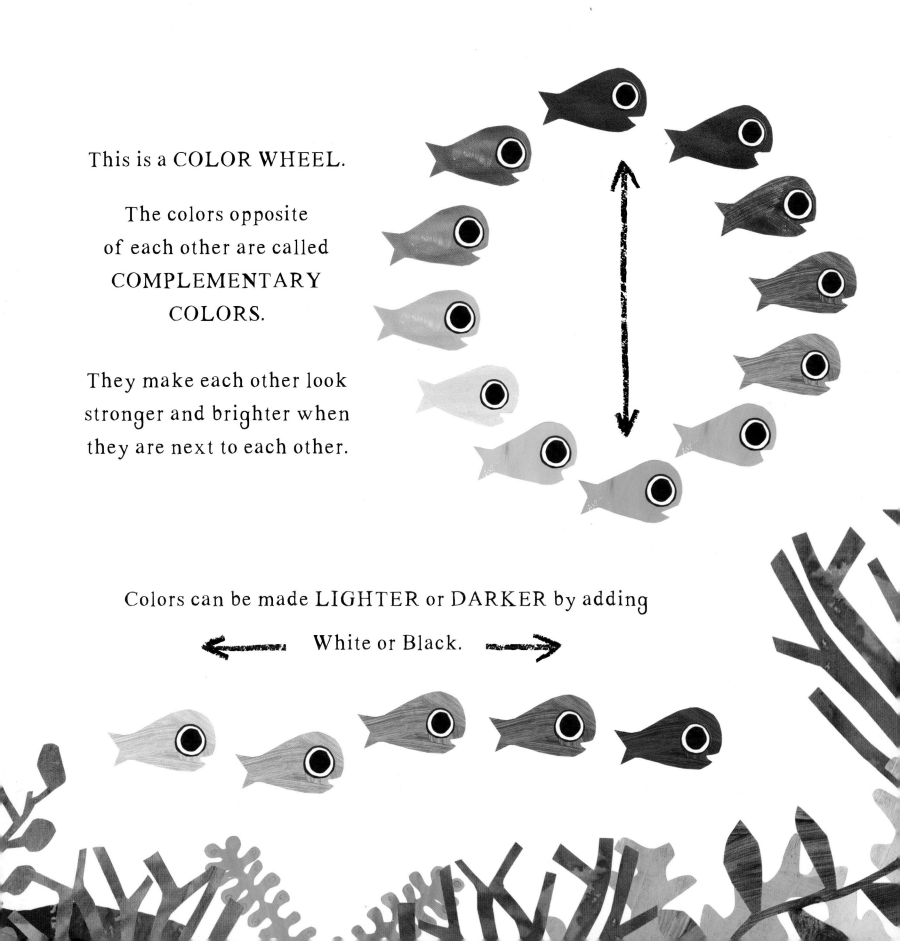

This is a COLOR WHEEL.

The colors opposite
of each other are called
COMPLEMENTARY
COLORS.

They make each other look
stronger and brighter when
they are next to each other.

Colors can be made LIGHTER or DARKER by adding

← White or Black. →